Here Comes Santa Claus

(Right Down Santa Claus Lane)

Words and Music by
GENE AUTRY
and OAKLEY HALDEMAN

A♭		A♮dim		E♭	C7	Fm	B♭7

Bells are ring - ing, chil - dren sing - sing, All is mer - ry and
Hear those sleigh - bells jin - gle jan - gle, What a beau - ti - ful
Sant - a knows that we're God's chil - dren— That makes ev - 'ry - thing—
Peace on earth will come to all If we just fol - low the

mf

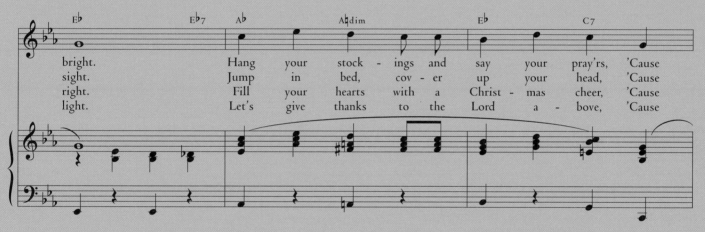

E♭	E♭7	A♭	A♮dim	E♭	C7

bright. Hang your stock - ings and say your pray'rs, 'Cause
sight. Jump in bed, cov - er up your head, 'Cause
right. Fill your hearts with a Christ - mas cheer, 'Cause
light. Let's give thanks to the Lord a - bove, 'Cause

1, 2, 3 Fm	B♭7	E♭ B♭7	4 Fm	B♭7	E♭

1.
2. { Sant - a Claus comes to - night.   4. Sant - a Claus comes to - night.
3.

Fine

ISBN 0-439-63779-1

Text copyright © 1947, 1970 by Gene Autry Music Publishing Inc.
Copyright assigned 1948 to Western Music Publishing Co.
Illustrations copyright © 2002 by Bruce Whatley. All rights reserved.
Published by Scholastic Inc., 557 Broadway, New York, NY 10012,
by arrangement with HarperCollins Publishers. SCHOLASTIC
and associated logos are trademarks and/or registered trademarks of Scholastic Inc.

12 11 10 9   6 7 8/0

Printed in the U.S.A.   40

First Scholastic printing, December 2003

Typography by Al Cetta

Here Comes Santa Claus

WORDS AND MUSIC
BY GENE AUTRY
AND OAKLEY HALDEMAN

ILLUSTRATED BY
BRUCE WHATLEY

SCHOLASTIC INC.
New York Toronto London Auckland Sydney
Mexico City New Delhi Hong Kong Buenos Aires

Here comes Santa Claus! Here comes Santa Claus!
Right down Santa Claus Lane!
Vixen and Blitzen and all his reindeer
Are pulling on the rein.

Bells are ringing, children singing,
All is merry and bright.

Hang your stockings and say your prayers,
'Cause Santa Claus comes tonight.

Here comes Santa Claus! Here comes Santa Claus!
Right down Santa Claus Lane!
He's got a bag that is filled with toys
For the boys and girls again.

Hear those sleigh bells jingle jangle,
What a beautiful sight.

Jump in bed, cover up your head,
'Cause Santa Claus comes tonight.

Here comes Santa Claus! Here comes Santa Claus!
Right down Santa Claus Lane!
He doesn't care if you're rich or poor
For he loves you just the same.

Santa knows that we're God's children—
That makes everything right.

Fill your hearts with a Christmas cheer,
'Cause Santa Claus comes tonight.

Here comes Santa Claus! Here comes Santa Claus!
Right down Santa Claus Lane!
He'll come around when the chimes ring out—
Then it's Christmas morn again.

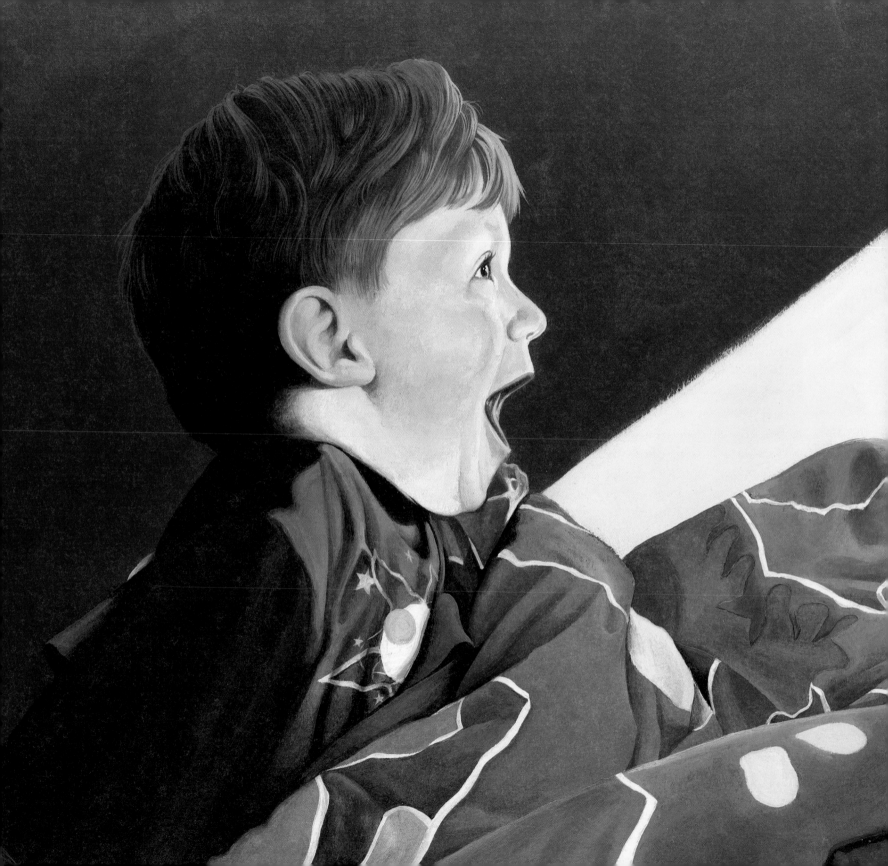

Peace on Earth will come to all
If we just follow the light.

Let's give thanks to the Lord above,
'Cause Santa Claus comes tonight!

Here Comes Santa Claus

(Right Down Santa Claus Lane)

Words and Music by
GENE AUTRY
and OAKLEY HALDEMAN

Here comes Sant-a Claus! Here comes Sant-a Claus! Right down Sant-a Claus Lane!

Vix - en and Blitz - en and all his rein - deer Are pull - ing on the rein.
He's got a bag that is filled with toys For the boys and girls a - gain.
He does - n't care if you're rich or poor For he loves you just the same.
He'll come a - round when the chimes ring out— Then it's Christ - mas morn a - gain.